THE SMALLEST KOALA

For my seven little Australians.   Gwen Mason

For all children who love our trees and our koalas.   Errol Broome

First published in 1987 by Buttercup Books Pty. Ltd,
281-A High Street, Ashburton, Victoria, 3147, Australia

© Text Errol Broome, 1987
© Illustrations Gwen Mason, 1987
ALL RIGHTS RESERVED
Typeset by Graphicset, Mitcham, Victoria
Printed and bound in Hong Kong by Colorcraft Ltd

National Library of Australia
Cataloguing-in-Publication entry
Broome, Errol
    The Smallest Koala
ISBN 0 949447 65 X
I. Koalas — Juvenile fiction. 1. Mason, Gwen, 1922-
II. Title.
A823'.3

THE SMALLEST KOALA

Story
Errol Broome

Illustrations
Gwen Mason

Buttercup

'Not gum leaves again,' said Kinta. 'Can't we ever have anything else?'

Her mother chewed a Manna leaf. 'Don't ask silly questions, Kinta. You know koalas only eat gum leaves.' She snapped a sprig of leaves from an overhanging branch. 'Here, eat your gum tips, Kinta.'

Kinta rubbed her leather patch nose. She was gazing through the eucalypts to the oak tree at the edge of the forest. 'Why can't we live in *that* tree?' she thought.

The oak tree was different from all other trees in the bush. In autumn, its leaves turned wondrous golds and reds and scattered at her feet. Its branches invited her to climb.

Surely, it was a magic tree. If only she could taste its leaves. While her mother dozed, Kinta hurried along the forest path.

As she climbed the oak tree, she forgot her mother's words.
'No, Kinta! You must never touch the oak leaves.'

She began to eat.

And as she ate, strange things happened. The forest started to sing. Music whirled inside Kinta's head and she tumbled to the ground.

When she opened her eyes, the sky was alive with colour. 'What big butterflies!' thought Kinta. 'What enormous butterflies!'

'So small, so small,' whistled the wind through the trees.

Kinta looked again. 'No, it's me!' she cried. 'I've shrunk!' for she had become no bigger than a butterfly. She was as small as the acorns that swung from the branches of the oak tree.

She wished she had never set eyes on that tree.

Plop, plop, plop. Kinta forgot the butterflies, for something was falling from the tree. From its branches sprang an army of acorn men.

'Hey, hey, who's been nibbling *our* leaves?'

Kinta hid her head, but the acorn men had spotted her. They waved their caps and leaped and stamped and prodded her with their fingertips. 'Hey, hey, what's this?'

Kinta rolled herself into a ball and bounced down the blossom
path. The acorn men scrambled after her.
'Hey, hey,' they sang. 'Follow that ball of fluff.'

'Ball of fluff, indeed!' cried Kinta. 'What nasty, rude men they are.'

Through rocky gullies they chased until Kinta ached with weariness.

'So small, so small,' sang choirs of dancing flowers. The rocks and flowers were strangers to her and Kinta knew then that she was lost. 'I want to go home,' she said.

But the acorn men kept coming.

Ahead, a friendly gum tree beckoned. 'Try me, try me,' sang its branches.

Kinta scratched her way up the trunk. She waved away the leaves, but let the gumnuts give her shelter. 'I'm safe here,' she said, for the acorn men did not belong in gum trees.

Below, the acorn men were searching. 'Where's that ball of fluff?'

Far away, the koalas were searching too. 'Where's Kinta?'

Kinta thought she would never see them again.

'So small, so small,' whistled the wind around her head. With one deep breath, it lifted her like a puff of gum blossom and swept her into the river.

Kinta spluttered and snatched at a floating gum leaf.
She hauled herself up as the leaf bobbed along in the tide.
'They won't catch me now,' she gasped.

But the acorn army was close behind.

Water rippled and sighed and swished their boat towards Kinta.

'Grab that ball of fluff!' they cried, as their boat surged forward.

'Hey, hey . . . pull . . . heave, hurry . . . hurry. . . .'

Kinta's leaf skimmed across the water. Ahead, the rapids thundered and crashed. Her leaf sailed faster. The current pulled her towards the falls. Faster. The edge was near.

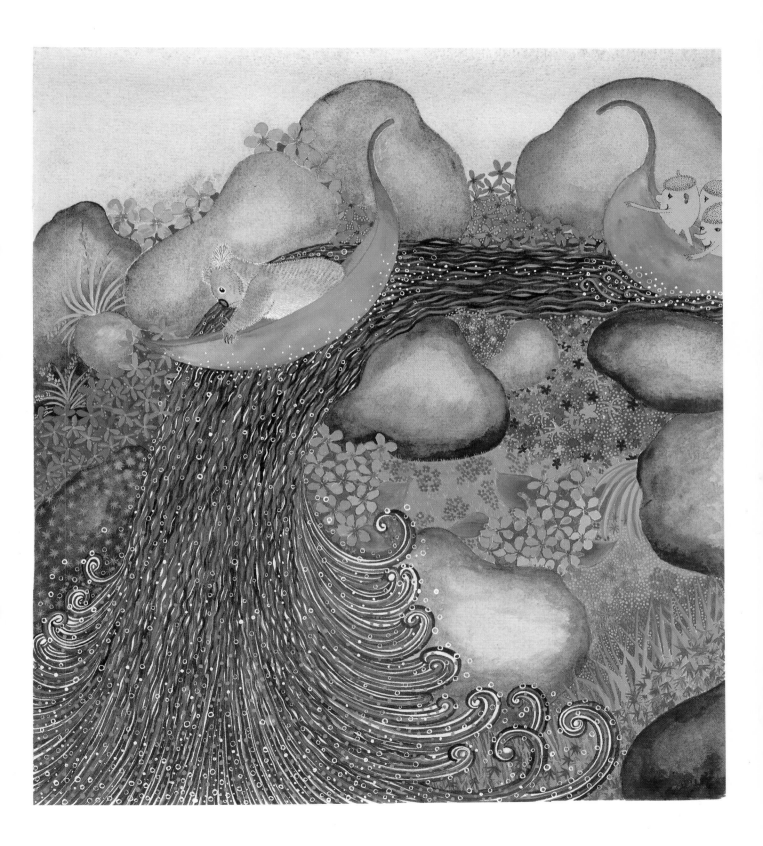

The leaf tipped and flung Kinta above the roaring foam. She clutched the air. Nothing. She was falling . . . . falling . . . . tossed in the wind until a lone gum blossom brushed against her cheek. Kinta reached out and grasped the stem. As she held it, the flower opened into a parachute and floated above the falls.

Below, she watched the acorn men sweeping towards the rapids.

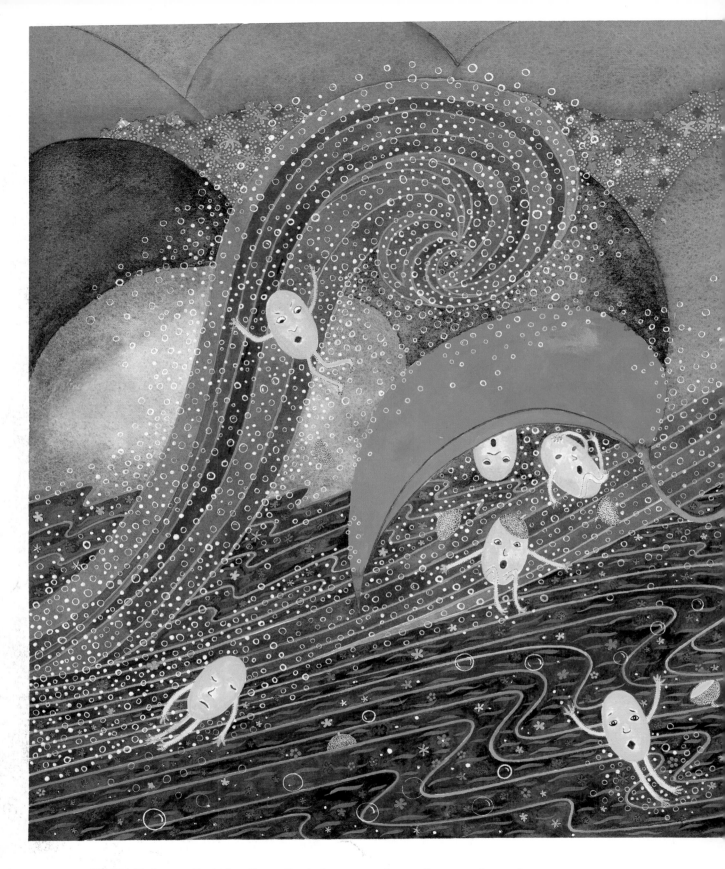

'Help!' they shrieked as their boat rocketed over the edge.
The acorn men scratched and clawed the air.

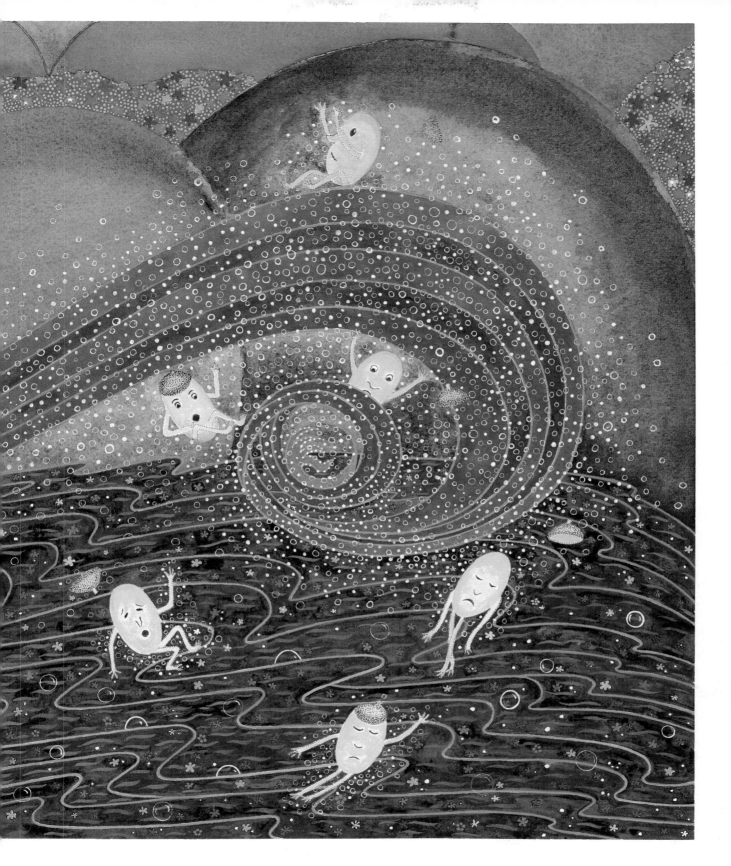

Glug, gulp. The swirling water swallowed them.

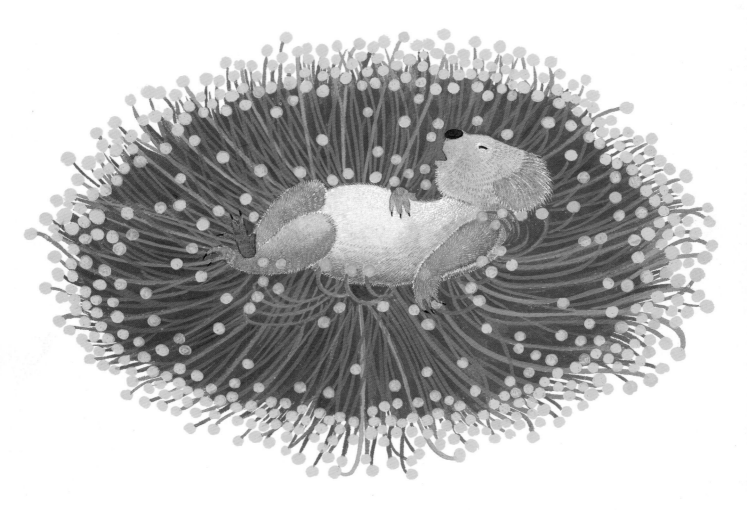

Kinta's parachute drifted across paddocks, above creeks and hills and homesteads.

'So small, so small,' chorused the clouds in the sky.

'And the world is so big,' thought Kinta, as the parachute whirled gently to the ground.

Exhausted, she slept at last.

When she woke up, she was hungry. Fern fronds tickled her nose. She stretched towards them.

. . . . No, Kinta. Her mother's words sounded in her ears.

Then perhaps some flowers would be nice? . . . . No, Kinta. Or oak leaves?

Never! If she hadn't eaten the oak leaves, she would be home now with her mother.

The eucalypts waved their leaves towards her.

Kinta rubbed her leather patch nose and said, 'They smell good to me.'

She nibbled the leaves and liked the taste. She ate more. And as she ate, the leaves looked smaller in her claws and the world did not seem so enormous.

Kinta was the right size again.

She was big enough now to find her own way home. She was big enough to laugh at acorn men, wherever they were.

The sky grew darker as she pushed through the bush towards the tallest gum in the forest. Through the trees, she heard the grunts of other koalas. 'Kinta, Kinta,' they called.

'I'm here,' she cried. 'I'm home.'

Stars lit their way to the gum tree.

'Kinta is back!' they sang. 'Kinta is safe!'

And they danced around the tree.

Mother Koala climbed the trunk and said that tonight they would have a feast. Nobody had to prepare it — the food was waiting on the branches.

There would never be anything but gum leaves. And Kinta didn't mind.